P9-CME-748

JACQUELINE WOODSON

illustrated by **E. B. LEWIS**

NANCY PAULSEN BOOKS · An Imprint of Penguin Group (USA) Inc.

That winter, snow fell on everything, turning the world a brilliant white.

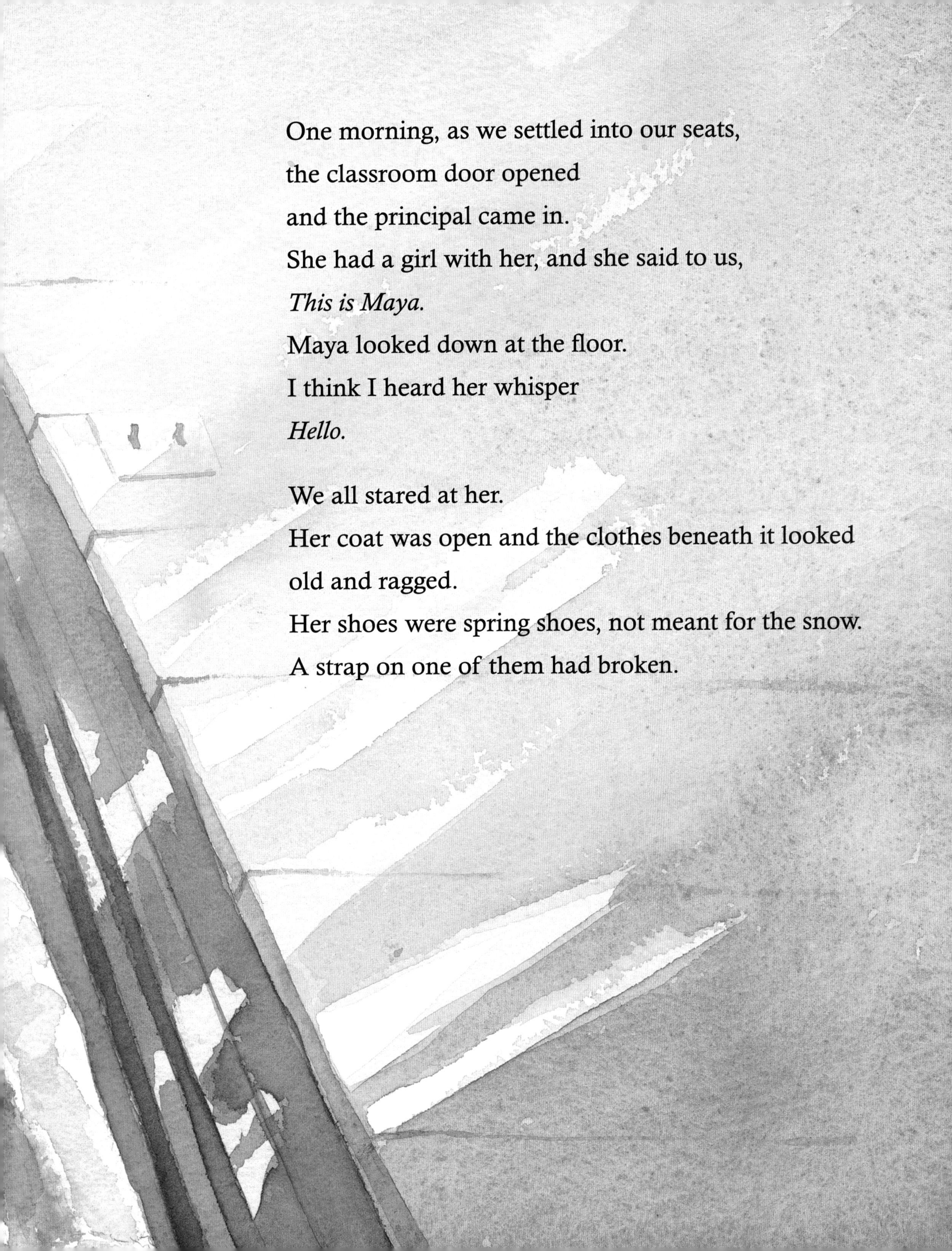

One morning, as we settled into our seats,
the classroom door opened
and the principal came in.
She had a girl with her, and she said to us,
This is Maya.
Maya looked down at the floor.
I think I heard her whisper
Hello.

We all stared at her.
Her coat was open and the clothes beneath it looked
old and ragged.
Her shoes were spring shoes, not meant for the snow.
A strap on one of them had broken.

Our teacher, Ms. Albert, said,
Say good morning to our new student.
But most of us were silent.

The only empty seat was next to me.
That's where our teacher put Maya.
And on that first day, Maya turned to me and smiled.
But I didn't smile back.
I moved my chair, myself and my books
a little farther away from her.
When she looked my way, I turned to the window
and stared out at the snow.

And every day after that,
when Maya came into the classroom,
I looked away and didn't smile back.

My best friends that year were Kendra and Sophie. At lunchtime, we walked around the school yard, our fingers laced together, whispering secrets into each other's ears.

One day, while we were near the slide,
Maya came over to us.
She held open her hand to show us
the shiny jacks and tiny red ball
she'd gotten for her birthday.
It's a high bouncer, she said.
But none of us wanted to play.

So Maya played a game against herself.

That afternoon, when we got back
into the classroom, Maya whispered to me,
Bet you can't guess who the new Jacks Champion of the World is.

Behind me, Andrew whispered,
Chloe's got a new friend. Chloe's got a new friend.

She's not my friend, I whispered back.

The weeks passed. Every day, we whispered about Maya, laughing at her clothes, her shoes, the strange food she brought for lunch.

Some days, Maya held out her hand to show us what she had brought to school— a deck of cards, pick up sticks, a small tattered doll.

Whenever she asked us to play, we said no.

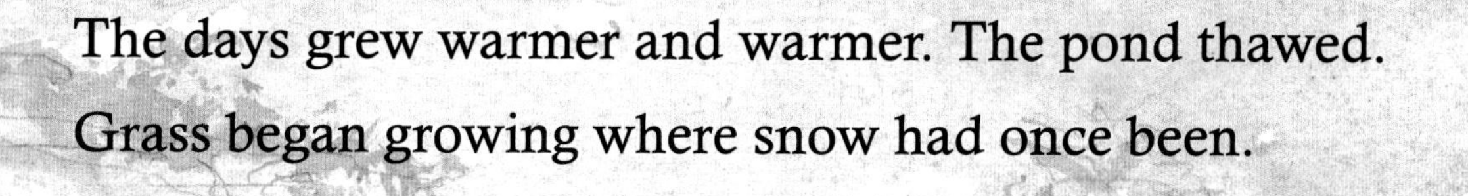

The days grew warmer and warmer. The pond thawed.
Grass began growing where snow had once been.

One day, Maya came to school wearing
a pretty dress and fancy shoes.
But the shoes and the dress looked like they'd
belonged to another girl before Maya.

I have a new name for her, Kendra whispered.
Never New.
Everything she has came from a secondhand store.

We all laughed. Maya stood by the fence.
She was holding a jump rope but did not come over
to us to ask if we wanted to play.
After a while, she folded it double, rolled the ends
around each hand and started jumping.
She jumped around the whole school yard
without stopping. She didn't look up once.
Just jumped, jumped, jumped.

The next day, Maya's seat was empty.
In class that morning, we were talking about kindness.

Ms. Albert had brought a big bowl into class and filled it with water. We all gathered around her desk and watched her drop a small stone into it. Tiny waves rippled out, away from the stone. *This is what kindness does,* Ms. Albert said. *Each little thing we do goes out, like a ripple, into the world.*

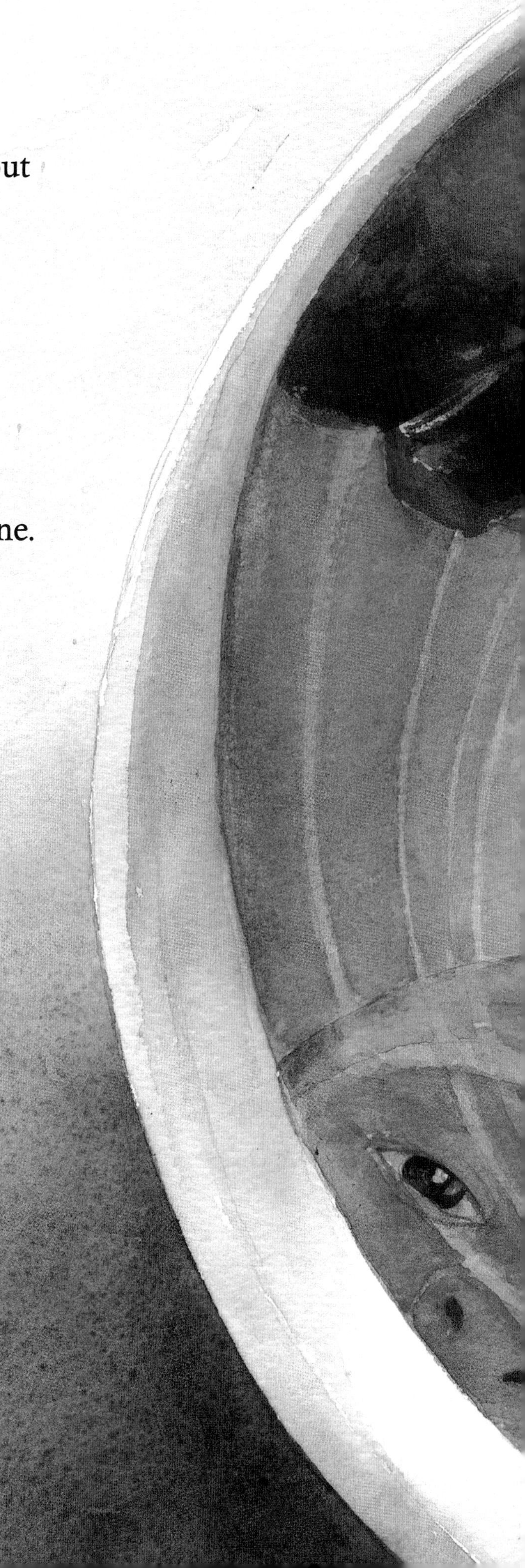

Then Ms. Albert let us each drop the stone
in as we told her
what kind things we had done.

Joseph had held the door for his grandmother.
Kendra helped change her baby brother's diaper.
Even mean old Andrew had done something.
I carried Teacher's books up the stairs, he said.
And Ms. Albert said it was true.

I stood there, holding Ms. Albert's rock
in my hand, silent.
Even small things count, Ms. Albert said gently.
But I couldn't think of anything and
passed the stone on.

Maya didn't come to school the next day. Or the day after that. Each morning, I walked to school slowly, hoping this would be the day Maya returned and she'd look at me and smile. I promised myself this would be the day I smiled back.

Each kindness, Ms. Albert had said,
makes the whole world a little bit better.

But Maya's seat remained empty.
And one day, Ms. Albert announced to the class
that Maya wouldn't be coming back.
Her family had to move away, Ms. Albert said.
Then she told us to take out our notebooks,
it was time for spelling.

That afternoon, I walked home alone.
When I reached the pond, my throat filled with
all the things I wished I would have said to Maya.
Each kindness I had never shown.

I threw small stones into it, over and over.
Watching the way the water rippled out and away.
Out and away.

Like each kindness—done and not done.
Like every girl somewhere—
holding a small gift out to someone
and that someone turning away from it.

I watched the water ripple
as the sun set through the maples
and the chance of a kindness with Maya
became more and more
forever gone.

To Angelina Mia, Ondina Kai and Ari Jazz—
with gratitude for each kindness.
—J. W.

To teacher Emily Goodman, her second-grade class,
and all of the students and staff at Haddonfield Friends School.
—E.B.L.

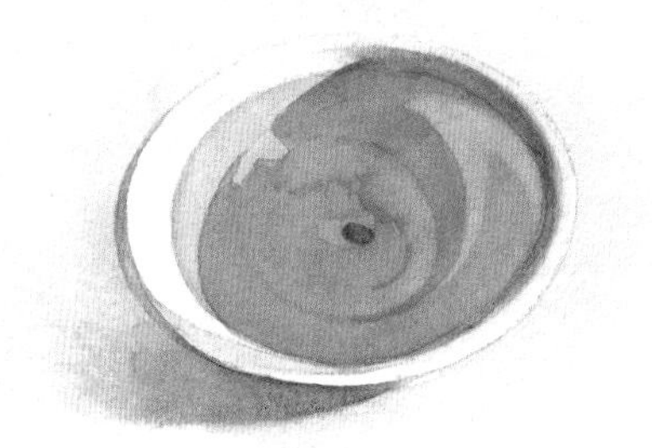

NANCY PAULSEN BOOKS
A division of Penguin Young Readers Group.
Published by The Penguin Group.
Penguin Group (USA) Inc., 375 Hudson Street, New York, NY 10014, U.S.A.
Penguin Group (Canada), 90 Eglinton Avenue East, Suite 700, Toronto, Ontario M4P 2Y3, Canada
(a division of Pearson Penguin Canada Inc.).
Penguin Books Ltd, 80 Strand, London WC2R 0RL, England.
Penguin Ireland, 25 St. Stephen's Green, Dublin 2, Ireland (a division of Penguin Books Ltd.).
Penguin Group (Australia), 250 Camberwell Road, Camberwell, Victoria 3124, Australia
(a division of Pearson Australia Group Pty Ltd).
Penguin Books India Pvt Ltd, 11 Community Centre, Panchsheel Park, New Delhi - 110 017, India.
Penguin Group (NZ), 67 Apollo Drive, Rosedale, Auckland 0632, New Zealand (a division of Pearson New Zealand Ltd).
Penguin Books (South Africa) (Pty) Ltd, 24 Sturdee Avenue, Rosebank, Johannesburg 2196, South Africa.
Penguin Books Ltd, Registered Offices: 80 Strand, London WC2R 0RL, England.

Published simultaneously in Canada. Manufactured in China by RR Donnelley Asia Printing Solutions Ltd.
Design by Ryan Thomann. Text set in Calisto. The art was done in watercolor on Arches paper.

Library of Congress Cataloging-in-Publication Data
Woodson, Jacqueline. Each kindness / Jacqueline Woodson ; illustrated by E. B. Lewis. p. cm.
Summary: When Ms. Albert teaches a lesson on kindness, Chloe realizes that she and her friends have been wrong in
making fun of new student Maya's shabby clothes and refusing to play with her.
[1. Kindness—Fiction. 2. Friendship—Fiction. 3. Schools—Fiction.] I. Lewis, Earl B., ill. II. Title.
PZ7.W84945Ea 2012 [E]—dc23 2011046800
ISBN 978-0-399-24652-4
22